Nate the Great
and the
Crunchy Christmas

Nate The Great
and the
Crunchy Christmas

by Marjorie Weinman Sharmat
and Craig Sharmat
illustrated by Marc Simont

A YEARLING BOOK

Text copyright © 1996 by Marjorie Weinman Sharmat and Craig Sharmat
Cover art and interior illustrations © 1996 by Marc Simont
Extra Fun Activities copyright © 2005 by Emily Costello
Extra Fun Activities illustrations copyright © 2005 by Jody Wheeler

All rights reserved. Published in the United States by Yearling, an imprint of
Random House Children's Books, a division of Penguin Random House LLC,
New York. Originally published in hardcover in the United States by Delacorte
Press, an imprint of Random House Children's Books, in 1996, and subsequently
published in paperback with Extra Fun Activities by Yearling, in 2005.

Yearling and the jumping horse design are registered trademarks of
Penguin Random House LLC.

Visit us on the Web! randomhousekids.com

Educators and librarians, for a variety of teaching tools, visit us at
RHTeachersLibrarians.com

Library of Congress Cataloging-in-Publication Data is available upon request.
ISBN 978-0-385-32117-4 (trade) — ISBN 978-0-440-41299-1 (pbk.) —
ISBN 978-0-385-37686-0 (ebook)

Printed in the United States of America
40   39   38   37   36   35

First Yearling Edition 2005

To my grandparents,
Nathan and Anna,
Leon and Lucille
—C.S.

I, Nate the Great,
am a detective.
I do important things.
Today I was doing something important.
I was shoveling snow.
My dog, Sludge, was chasing snowflakes.
Suddenly I heard a jingling sound.

1

Annie was coming up our walk
with her dog, Fang.
Fang had bells on his collar
and an elf hat on his head.
"Doesn't Fang look cute?" Annie said.
"Just like a giant elf."

Sludge looked at me.
I looked at Sludge.
We both knew that all
the bells and elves
and jingles and jangles
in the world
could not make Fang
look cute.
Fang looked hungry.
"Fang is not a happy elf,"
Annie said.
This was not good news.
"Every year, two weeks before
Christmas, Fang gets a
Christmas card from his mother
in the mail," Annie said.
"It is now a week
before Christmas

and Fang has not received
his card."
"Perhaps she didn't send it,"
I said.
"Would a mother forget Fang?"
Annie said.
I, Nate the Great,
wished I could.
"I need your help
to find the card,"
Annie said.
"I have to shovel snow,"
I said.
Fang sat down and glared at me.
I, Nate the Great,
was thinking.
It was the holiday season.

It was not a good idea
for a giant elf
to be unhappy.
"I will take your case,"
I said. "Wait here."
I went into my house.
I wrote a note to my mother.

Dear Mother,
I stopped shoveling
snow.
I am on a case for
a giant elf.
The snow won't go
away. Neither will
The elf. I will be back.
Love
Nate the Great

I went outside.
I spoke to Annie.
"The mailman leaves your mail
in your mailbox, right?"
"Most of the time," Annie said.
"Sometimes he drops it
on the ground
near the mailbox."

"Why does he do that?"
"Sometimes Fang is
so happy to see
the mailman that he
runs out of the house
to greet him.
The mailman drops the mail
and flees."
I, Nate the Great, knew
exactly how the mailman felt.
I said, "Then what?"
"Fang runs after the mailman.
They both disappear.
I run out to get the mail."
"So, there is no chance
for anybody else
to take that mail?"

"No chance," Annie said.
"We must go to your mailbox
and look for clues," I said.
Annie, Fang, Sludge, and I
walked through the snow.
It was crunchy under our feet.
"Are you missing any other mail?"
I asked.
"No," Annie said.

I walked up to Annie's mailbox.
It was so stuffed
that pieces of mail
were sticking out.
"I guess that today's mail
came while I was at your house,"
Annie said.
I started to open the mailbox.
"Watch out!" Annie yelled.

It was too late.
What must have been
the largest single-day collection
of holiday catalogs
of holiday catalogs
ever mailed to one address
landed on me.
This was not going to be
an easy case.
"How long have you
been getting these catalogs?"
I asked.
"For about eight weeks.
I collect them," Annie said.
"I haven't had a chance
to read most of them yet.
Last year I counted
one billion nine hundred

and ninety-nine things
that you could buy."
I, Nate the Great,
did not want to know
what any of them were.
But the catalogs could be
a clue.

"I need to see the catalogs
that came last week," I said.
"About the time that Fang's card
should have arrived."
"My catalogs are all mixed up,"
Annie said. "They are in my room."
Annie, Fang, Sludge, and I
went to Annie's room.
One whole side of it was
covered with catalogs.
This was going to be
a long day.
I walked over and picked up
a catalog.

I started to look
through the pages.
An envelope fell out.
I picked it up.

"This looks like your
heating bill," I said.
"Didn't you miss getting it?"
Annie shrugged.
"It's never addressed
to me or Fang. So it
doesn't count."
I flipped through
more pages.
A postcard fell out.
It was addressed to Fang.
But I, Nate the Great,
did not think that
Fang would want to see it.
It was a reminder
from the vet
for Fang to come in
for his shots.

I picked up another catalog.
I found three envelopes in
that one.
I spoke to Annie.
"I have solved your case."
"Oh, great," Annie said.
"So where is Fang's card?"
"Solving is one thing.

Finding is another,"
I said. "The card
must be somewhere in your
catalogs. A lot of your mail
got stuck inside them.
I hope that we won't
have to look through
one billion nine hundred
and ninety-nine things
before we find the card."
Annie and I looked
through one catalog

after another.
Sludge sniffed each one.
Some of the catalogs
were for dogs.
Christmas food for dogs.
Christmas toys for dogs.
Christmas clothes for dogs.
Fang must be on a mailing list.

Envelopes kept dropping out.
But none were from Mrs. Fang.
At last I said,
"I have not solved this case.
I need clues.
Do you still have the old cards
Fang got from his mother?"
"Oh yes, Fang saves them,"
Annie said. "Here are the ones
from the last three years."
I looked at the cards.
The one from the first year
was tiny. It said
"Merry Christmas from Mother Fang.
May you eat lots of doggie bones
and grow."
The card must have worked.

The card from the second year
was bigger.
It said "Merry Christmas
from Mother Fang.
Are you eating your bones, son?
A bone a day
keeps the vet away."

The third card was even bigger.
It said "Merry Christmas from
Mother Fang.
Wear your booties in the snow.
Don't go out when it's ten below.
Eat those bones and grow, grow, grow!"
"Mrs. Fang is such a bossy mother!"
Annie said. "She knows Fang
loves bones anyway."

"Let me get this straight,"
I said. "Fang is happy
to get these cards?"
"Oh yes," Annie said.
"On Christmas Day
he jumps up on my lap.
I read him the card.
He listens to every word."
"He jumps on your *lap*?" I said.
"And he snuggles," Annie said.
"Maybe that's a clue?"
"Maybe that's a miracle,"
I said.
I, Nate the Great, was thinking.
The cards got bigger each year.
So this year's card
must be the biggest yet.
It should be easy to find.

"Who else was here last week
when the mail came?" I asked.
"Rosamond and her four cats,"
Annie said. "She was looking
for a cat catalog."
"Did you get one?"
"Yes, and I gave it to her."
"Aha! So Rosamond has
one of your catalogs.
I must go to her house."
Sludge and I left.
We crunched our way
to Rosamond's house.
On her front door
there was a big card
with a poem
and a picture of a cat
with a red cap

Santa Claws,
My cats do Too.
A scriTchy-scraTchy
(hrisTmas) To you

and a white beard.
I could tell that
Rosamond was going to have
a very strange Christmas.
I knocked on the door.
Rosamond answered it.
"You are just in time
to help me decorate
my cat tree," she said.

Sludge and I walked inside.
The tree was in the
middle of the living room.
There were tuna fish cans
painted red and green
hanging from it.
All of Rosamond's cats
were sitting in the tree.
On the bottom branch was
Super Hex.
On the next branch was Big Hex.
On the next branch was Plain Hex.
On the top branch was Little Hex.
He had a ribbon around his neck
with a star hanging from it.
Rosamond smiled.
"Little Hex is the star
of my tree."

"A fine choice," I said.
"I have come to see
your cat catalog."
"Here it is,"
Rosamond said.

CAT
CATALOG
999
THINGS
TO GIVE
YOUR CAT
for CHRISTMAS

I flipped through the pages.
"What are you looking for?"
Rosamond asked.
"A big Christmas card
from Fang's mother to Fang.
But it is not in here."
"That's dog stuff," Rosamond
said. "You won't find it in
a CATalog." Rosamond laughed.
Then she said, "I did find something.
I think it's a telephone bill."
"I will give it to Annie,"
I said. "Pretty soon she will
have no heat and no phone service.
Only catalogs."
Sludge and I walked toward the door.
"Wait, my tree isn't finished,"
Rosamond said.

"It looks finished to me," I said.
"I wish you and your cats
a Merry Christmas."
Sludge and I headed for home.
I had to think about the case.
Pancakes help me think.
At home I made potato pancakes.
I eat them every Chanukah.
"Happy Chanukah, Sludge," I said.
I gave Sludge his card
and a bone.
Sludge wagged his tail,
sniffed the card,
and started to eat the bone.

Crunch! Munch! Crunch!
"You are having a crunchy
Chanukah," I said. "Do
you know what *I* want
for the holiday?"
Sludge looked up.
"*Clues!*" I said.
I was thinking,
Do I have *any*?

I knew a lot of facts.
But were they *clues*?
I knew that Fang's card
was big.
I knew that when Fang
greeted the mailman
he dropped the mail
and ran for his life.
I knew that Annie had a strong lap.
Forget that one.
I knew that Rosamond had
the world's strangest
Christmas tree.
Forget that one too.
I knew that Mrs. Fang
was a bossy mother.
She kept after Fang
to eat bones.

But dogs love bones anyway.
I looked at Sludge.
He kept making crunching sounds
with his bone.
Hmm.
Was he trying to tell me something?
He was.
He knew what I had to do
to solve this case.
He knew that I, Nate the Great,
had to think like a dog!
I did not want to do that.
But I had to find the card.
"Come," I said to Sludge.
Sludge and I rushed back
to Annie's house.
It was hard to do.

The snow was getting
deeper and deeper.
I handed the telephone bill
to Annie. Then I said,
"There is a clue in
Fang's old Christmas cards.
Each year the cards
got bigger.
But that's not the clue.
Each year Mrs. Fang
got bossier.

She sent stronger messages
for Fang to eat bones.
That's a clue."
"So where is this year's
message?" Annie asked.
"I, Nate the Great, say
that Fang has it."
"Fang?"
"Yes. He found the envelope
on the ground
next to the mailbox."
Annie looked at Fang.
"I knew you were
a very smart dog," she said.
"But I didn't know that
you knew how to read."

"He doesn't," I said.
"But he knows how to sniff
and to hide things.
Tell me, does he have
a favorite hiding place?"
"Yes. Somewhere in
the backyard," Annie said.
"Follow me," I said.
Annie, Fang, and Sludge
followed me to the backyard.

It was covered with snow.

There was no trail.

"Look for a hump
or bump
in the snow," I said.

"It might be covering a hump
or bump of dirt
where Fang dug."

"I see one over there," Annie said.

"We must dig there," I said.

Annie and I started to dig.

Fang and Sludge watched.

"Why are *we* digging?" Annie asked.

"Isn't that what *dogs* do?"

I stared at Annie.

"Dig," I said.

Annie and I dug up a ball.

A shoe.

And a big, thick, soggy envelope.

"Hey, it has Fang's name on it!"

Annie said.

She handed it to Fang.

Fang tore open the envelope.

There was a bone inside.

With a card tied to it.
It said "Merry Christmas from
Mother Fang. *Eat!*"
"I, Nate the Great,
say that every year
Mrs. Fang told
Fang to eat bones.
Her message got stronger.
At last she sent Fang . . .
a real bone!

It must have come on a day
when Fang greeted the mailman.
The mail fell to the ground.
Fang sniffed the envelope.
He knew what was inside.
He ran off with it
and buried it in the dirt.
Then the snow covered it.
We uncovered it.
Now Fang will have
a crunchy Christmas.
Case solved."
Annie looked at Fang.
"You naughty elf.
You made us look
for the card
and you were hiding it
all this time."

Annie looked at me.
"Maybe this is what
elves do at Christmas time."
"No," I said. "This is
what dogs do all the time."
"How did you figure
that out?" Annie asked.
"I, Nate the Great, had to
think like a . . . detective,"
I said.
I turned to leave.
This was the last time
I would take a case
for a gigantic elf.
An elf who did not need me
in the first place.
An elf who already knew

what it took me
three and one half hours
to find out.
Suddenly the elf
dropped his bone.
Maybe he knew that
Christmas was not
until next week.
He rushed up to me.
He started to lick me.

He jingled while he licked.
"He's saying 'Happy Holidays,' "
Annie said.
"He's saying *'I'm hungry,'* " I said.
"Give this hardworking elf
an extra bone
so he can save his mother's
for Christmas."
Sludge and I started to walk away.
"Fang will love you forever," Annie said.

Sludge and I walked faster.

We headed home.

Snow was still falling.

Three and one half hours of it.

To shovel.

Maybe it would melt if I waited.

A month.

Sludge and I went up our walk.

Candles were shining in the window.

It was time for one more card . . .

~Extra~
Fun Activities!

What's Inside

NATE'S NOTES: Snowfall

Rochester, New York, is a good place to live if you like shoveling. The city gets about ninety-four inches of snow every winter. It is the snowiest large city in the United States. Runner-up: Buffalo, New York.

Every state in the U.S. gets snow occasionally. It even snows in Florida and on the volcanic mountains in Hawaii.

In 1862, cities began using snowplows to clear city streets. Horses pulled the plows. Motorized plows arrived about 1913.

Snow and trains don't mix. In the late 1800s, engineers built the first rapid transit trains in New York City. The trains rode on tracks high above the sidewalk. The trains were called the Elevated—or the El, for short.

Being up high was supposed to keep the trains safe from snowdrifts. However, in 1888, a huge blizzard covered the tracks. After that, New York put its trains underground. In 1904, the subway was born! Some of the elevated tracks are still in use, though.

NATE'S NOTES: Types of Snow

Not all snow is the same. Here are a few different types of snow. Can you think of more?

POWDER—A "dry" snow that doesn't pack easily. Good for skiing. Not good for snowballs, since it doesn't hold together well.

SLUSH—A very wet snow. Not good for much except soaking through your boots.

SUGAR—Snow shaped like tiny pebbles.

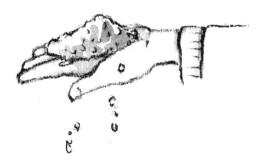

STICKY—The kind of snow that sticks together. Perfect for making snowmen and snow forts.

When temperatures drop below zero, snow on the ground will squeak as you walk over it. The colder the air, the louder the squeak!

Snowflakes form in clouds around tiny specks of dust. In places where the soil is red, the snow can be pink!

Scientists say snowflakes always have six sides. And it's true that no two snowflakes are alike. Test it out. On a snowy day, slip on a pair of navy or black gloves. Go outside. Catch a few snowflakes. How many sides do they have? Are any of the flakes alike?

NATE'S NOTES:
Christmas Catalogs

Annie gets a lot of catalogs.
Nate learned that she isn't alone.

Each year, stores mail about 17 billion catalogs. That's about 59 catalogs for every man, woman, and child in the United States. Altogether, the catalogs weigh about 3.6 million tons.

Why do stores mail so many catalogs? Each year, people buy more than $100 billion worth of stuff from them.

Letter carriers say delivering the mail in November is hard work. That's when most of the Christmas catalogs arrive. Some come as early as July.

9

Six Fun Things to Do
on a Snowy Day

Making a snowman is nice. Sledding is fun. Nate poked around. He uncovered a few more things to do in the cold and snow:

1. **Snow paintings:** Fill a squirt bottle with water and a few drops of food coloring. Use the squirt to create words and drawings on fresh, clean snow. If you have several bottles, you can use different colors to make more complicated designs.

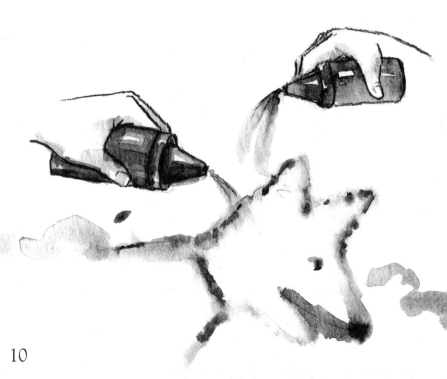

2. **Snow turtle:** Fill a mixing bowl with clean snow. Pack well. Dump out. Use a sand shovel or spoon to carve out a head, feet, and a tail. Spray with green water (see #1). Other shapes to try: a castle, a pyramid, and a spaceship.

3. Scout for tracks: Visit the library or go online to learn about animal tracks.* Now practice your detective skills. Carefully search your backyard or a nearby park for tracks. Can you identify any? Make sketches of your findings. Keep them in a notebook.

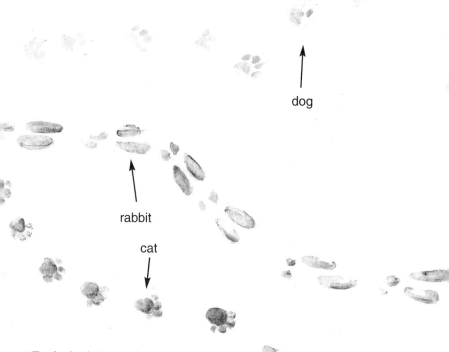

dog

rabbit

cat

* Try this book: *Big Tracks, Little Tracks: Following Animal Tracks*, by Millicent E. Selsam. And check out the Animal Track Identification Guide at this Web site: www.studyworksonline.com/creating_dinos/AT1.pdf

4. **Blow bubbles:** Mix together 2 tablespoons dish soap, 3 cups warm water, and 2 tablespoons glycerin.* Go outside and blow bubbles. (If you don't have a bubble wand, try using straws, a small funnel, or cookie cutters.) On a cold day, warm bubbles fly up into the sky. Extremely cold air will freeze bubbles solid. Frozen bubbles will land on the ground without breaking. They may last several minutes before popping.

* Look for glycerin at the drugstore.

5. **Make snow ice cream:** On the same day as a big snowfall, collect some clean snow. Mix together 3 cups snow, 2 tablespoons milk, ¼ cup sugar, and 1 teaspoon vanilla extract. Eat it up!

6. **Target practice:** Make a bunch of snowballs. Prop a plastic "saucer" sled up in the snow. Use masking tape to make several circles, target-style, on the saucer. Award five points for hitting the saucer, five points for an outer ring, and twenty-five points for a bull's-eye.

How to Make Potato Pancakes

Potato pancakes are good for Chanukah. Potato pancakes are just plain good. Try them. You'll see. Even better: potato pancakes with applesauce. (Applesauce recipe starts on page 19.)

Ask an adult to help with this recipe.
Makes four servings.

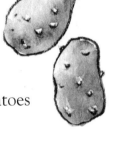

GET TOGETHER:

- a large mixing bowl
- a spoon
- 4 cups of frozen shredded potatoes or hash brown mix
- 2 large eggs
- 1 teaspoon salt
- a dash of black pepper
- 2 tablespoons flour or matzo meal
- 1 teaspoon baking powder
- vegetable oil for frying
- a frying pan
- a spatula
- paper towels
- applesauce
- sour cream

MAKE YOUR POTATO PANCAKES:

1. Use the spoon to mix the potatoes, eggs, salt, pepper, flour or matzo meal, and baking powder together in the bowl. The mixture should be gloppy.
2. Coat the bottom of the pan with oil. Heat on medium-high heat until bubbling.

3. Carefully spoon 2 tablespoons of batter into the oil. Flatten with the spoon.
4. Cook for about 4 minutes until golden brown and crisp.
5. Use the spatula to flip the pancakes. Be careful not to splatter oil.
6. Cook 4 more minutes.

7. Remove from the pan. Place on paper towels to absorb extra oil.
8. Continue to fry pancakes until the batter is gone. Add more oil to the pan when you need it.
9. Serve with applesauce and sour cream.

How to Make Applesauce

Applesauce goes well with potato pancakes. You can also eat it plain.

Ask an adult to help with this recipe.
Makes six servings.

GET TOGETHER:

- six apples
- ½ cup water
- ¼ cup sugar
- a peeler
- a sharp knife
- a spoon
- a saucepan with a lid
- 1 teaspoon cinnamon

MAKE YOUR APPLESAUCE:

1. Peel the apples. Cut away the seeds and the core.
2. Cut into chunks.
3. Put the apples, water, and sugar into a saucepan.
4. Bring to a boil. Reduce heat to low. Cover.
5. Cook for 30 minutes, or until the apples are soft.
6. Remove from the heat. Stir in the cinnamon. Let cool.
7. Eat!

How to Make Greeting Cards

Cold from playing outside? Come inside and make some cards. You can send them to friends for Christmas or Chanukah.

SUPPLIES:

- colored construction paper
- a ruler
- scissors
- markers, crayons, or colored pencils
- a glue stick
- artwork*
- a heavy book (like the phone book)
- envelopes

* Ask your parents first. Make sure they don't want to keep your paintings and drawings.

MAKE YOUR CARDS:

1. Using the ruler, trace a 12³⁄₄-by-6-inch rectangle onto your paper.
2. Cut it out.
3. Use the ruler to divide the paper into thirds. Each third will measure 4¹⁄₄ inches by 6 inches.

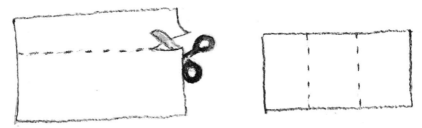

4. Fold the paper into thirds like this: Fold one end piece over the middle. Flip the card over, and fold the other end piece over the middle. The card should open like an accordion.

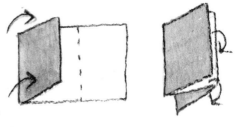

5. From the top third, cut out a window that will fit your artwork. Leave about a ¹⁄₂-inch border around the edges.

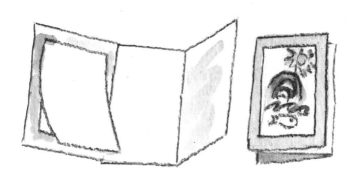

6. Slip the artwork behind the window. Glue the back of the artwork to the frame. Glue the frame to the middle piece of paper. You should still have a flap that opens like a greeting card.

7. Place the card under the heavy book for about an hour.

8. After the glue is dry, use the pencils or markers to write a holiday greeting inside.

9. Put the card in the envelope and mail.

How to Make Dog Biscuits

Sludge and Fang like biscuits that look like bones. If you have a dog, he or she probably likes them too. Why not make some?

Ask an adult to help you with this recipe. Makes about two dozen dog biscuits (depending on the size of your cookie cutter).

GET TOGETHER:

- ¹/₃ cup margarine
- ³/₄ cup hot water
- a large bowl
- ¹/₂ cup powdered milk

- 1 teaspoon salt
- 1 egg, beaten
- 3 cups whole wheat flour
- a bone-shape cookie cutter
- a cookie sheet

MAKE YOUR DOG BISCUITS:

1. Put the margarine in the bowl.
2. Pour the hot water over the margarine.
3. Stir in the powdered milk, salt, and egg.
4. Add the flour, ½ cup at a time.
5. On a table or counter, knead the dough for a few minutes, until it's stiff.
6. Pat the dough out on the counter until it is ½ inch thick.

7. Cut into bone shapes.
8. Bake at 325 degrees for 50 minutes.
9. Cool. The biscuits will get quite hard and look like the ones you buy at the supermarket.

Feed to your dog. (It's okay to taste them too—if you're curious.)

A word about learning with

Nate the Great

The Nate the Great series is good fun and has been entertaining children for over forty years. These books are also valuable learning tools in and out of the classroom.

Nate's world—his home, his friends, his neighborhood—is one that every young person recognizes. Nate introduces beginning readers and those who have graduated to early chapter books to the detective mystery genre, and they respond to Nate's commitment to solving the case and helping his friends.

What's more, as Nate the Great solves his cases, readers learn with him. Nate unravels mysteries by using evidence collection, cogent reasoning, problem-solving, analytical skills, and logic in a way that teaches readers to develop critical-thinking abilities. The stories help children start discussions about how to approach difficult situations and give them tools to resolve them.

When you read a Nate the Great book with a child, or when a child reads a Nate the Great mystery on his or her own, the child is guaranteed a satisfying ending that will have taught him or her important classroom and life skills. We know that you and your children will enjoy reading and learning from Nate the Great's wonderful stories as much as we do.

Find out more at NatetheGreatBooks.com.

Happy reading and learning with Nate!

Solve all the mysteries with

Nate the Great

MARJORIE WEINMAN SHARMAT has written more than 130 books for children and young adults, as well as movie and TV novelizations. Her books have been translated into twenty-four languages. The award-winning Nate the Great series, hailed in *Booklist* as "groundbreaking," has resulted in Nate's real-world appearances in many *New York Times* crossword puzzles, sporting a milk mustache in magazines and posters, residing on more than 28 million boxes of Cheerios, and touring the country in musical theater. Marjorie Weinman Sharmat and her husband, Mitchell Sharmat, have also coauthored many books, including titles in both the Nate the Great and the Olivia Sharp series.

CRAIG SHARMAT is a Los Angeles–based author, composer, and guitarist. His extensive credits include national television programs, feature films, and jingles. He is the coauthor of several Nate the Great books.

MARC SIMONT won the Caldecott Medal for his artwork in *A Tree Is Nice* by Janice May Udry, as well as a Caldecott Honor for his own book, *The Stray Dog*. He illustrated the first twenty books in the Nate the Great series.